A toy for Timmy

by Joel Biggs

Illustrated by:
Ginalyn Tirando

Daddy's taking little Timmy to the toy store to buy him a toy

To show how happy he is because
Timmy is such a good little boy

Timmy gets to choose one
Anything in the store

From the things on the shelves

To anything on the floor

But Timmy's not real sure
On which toy he should pick

Should be the big red ball

Or the really tall pogo stick

Should he choose the bag of marbles

Or the puzzles with all the trees

It's really tough to pick a toy
When you can have anyone you please

Maybe he'll get the squirt gun

Or a really cool guitar

Maybe he'll get the train set

The one with all the cars

Maybe he'll get the toy

That lets him spin around

Or a really cool guitar

Maybe he'll get the train set

The one with all the cars

Maybe he'll get the toy

That lets him spin around

Maybe he'l get the tunnel

That he can crawl through on the ground

He looks real close at the skates

Because he knows they'll make him fast

He knows all the toys by heart now

But he wants one that will really last

He really likes the drum set

Then again look at that bike

But finally he decides

Today he wants a kite...